frog, where are you?

by mercer mayer

dial books for young readers
new york

For Phyllis Fogelman,
a dear friend, who inspired
the creation of the faded
pink dummy

Published by Dial Books for Young Readers
A division of Penguin Putnam Inc.
345 Hudson Street
New York, New York 10014

24